VIRGINIA HAMILTON

A NOVEL

SCHOLASTIC  SIGNATURE

AN IMPRINT OF SCHOLASTIC INC.

NEW YORK   TORONTO   LONDON   AUCKLAND   SYDNEY
MEXICO CITY   NEW DELHI   HONG KONG   BUENOS AIRES

This book was originally published in hardcover by the Blue Sky Press in 1999.

ISBN 0-439-36786-7

12 11 10 9 8 7 6   3 4 5 6 7/0

Printed in the U.S.A.   40

First Scholastic paperback printing, February 2002

To the wonderful fifth grade, to teacher Judy Davis,

and to principal Shelley Harwayne, all at PS 290,

Manhattan New School, New York City.

Thanks for showing me your school,

for the rousing discussions of my book project,

and for graciously answering my many questions.

You are an inspiration.

Thanks go to Jaime Levi Adoff,

founder of Blueish Music.

He generously provided the word and its fine points,

which gave me the idea for this book.

J O U R N A L

The First Time I Saw Her

Bluish. In school.

She was there with her puppy. Nobody brings a dog to school! It was right in her arms.

Plus, some kids knew her. I didn't and Tuli didn't.

This girl wears a hat, like half a bowl. Sometimes, trying to stand up and walk.

Ms. Baker said, "Natalie, do as much as you feel like. Don't try to do everything."

Natalie is this girl's name. But that's not what kids call her. Call her Bluish and grin and look at her hard. Bluish fits her. This girl is like moonlight. So pale you see the blue veins all over. You can tell though, once she had some color.

I watch her all the time. She looks real tired. And lets the puppy sit on the floor. It's all black as night. She said its name. Bucky? I didn't get it. No! Its name is Lucky.

Never seen anyone like her up close. This girl.

Bluish closes her eyes. Her hands look like moonlight fishes about to dive and flop off the arms of her wheelchair.

Bluish: Another Day

After recess, Bluish sat outside of the classroom. Right in the middle of the hall. So when the buzzer rang we all had to go around her in her chair.

Some boy tried to push her but it was braked I guess. The chair didn't move.

The pushing all of a sudden made her jump like somebody hit her. Her eyes got real big. I was there.

Started to say: You want me to move you over?
But I said: You want me to bring you inside the
classroom?

She was looking at me very tough.

"I'm sitting right here until they look at me!"
That's what she said too. Because everybody is pretending not to see her.

She has all these nerves that jiggle her. Her
voice is squeaky. Never saw a kid with a teeny
mouth like hers. Little line mouth upside-down
smile. Makes her look like she's about to bawl.

Bluish: And Next

Outside. Today I almost fell on the sidewalk. Twice.
Black ice. But this is not about me.

She was outside, too. Bluish.

Do I tell Mom about this girl?

She gets on one of the small school buses. I
think maybe she comes from across town. She got
on the bus with her puppy. A lift rode them up and
the driver pulled her chair inside.

I like her hats. Different one today. Blue velvet.

This journal, excuse my mistakes. This is not for school. I'm not looking for a grade. Just all about Bluish.

I *love* her puppy.

CHAPTER ONE

Dreenie

"Whoop!" Dreenie yelled above the street noise.

She and her little sister were slipping, then sliding, as Dreenie picked their way along the icy sidewalk.

School was out for the day. Bunches of kids, talking loud, were heading over to Broadway.

Bluish.

Like a streak going through Dreenie, reminding her. Pale, glowing, fluttery, was the picture in her mind.

All around, brakes screeched and horns blasted. Cars and taxis slid through the slush.

Bluish.

Dreenie blinked into the hard bits of snow that hit her face. She shouldered her way through throngs of shoppers. Not quite shoving, but pushing through crowds of students and neighborhood folks. Seeing all the holiday decorations up and down Amsterdam Avenue.

Older women of the neighborhood with their shopping carts acted afraid they would be pushed. They went so slow! Dreenie eased around them so her little sister wouldn't tumble into them.

That had happened before. One woman had looked frightened, even though Dreenie had said she was sorry.

Dreenie was muscled and tall for her age. She often looked angry, even when she was not. She could pretend to be really tough. The woman had clutched her purse. It made Dreenie and her little sister feel bad, that someone would think they'd take what didn't belong to them. Worst was seeing Willeva's hurt face.

It was Dreenie's job to keep everything even. Keep Willeva—everybody called her Willie—in place right next to her.

Good, Dreenie thought. *Finished with school for the day.* She counted the days until holiday time. Not far off now. A couple of weeks. And she took hold of Willie by her coat sleeve, pulling her along.

"Let go of me, Drain!" Willie hollered, trying to break loose. "Who do you think you are, Drain?"

"Don't call me that!" Dreenie warned.

"I know who your mama *ain't*, Drain," Willie cried. "Because you sure *ain't* one of us Anneva and Gerald Browns! *Drain!*"

"One more time," Dreenie warned again. "And stop with the *ain't*." *Why is she such a pain?*

She and Willie went to the same school and were two grades apart. Lucky to transfer in, a quarter of the way, with school already started. Her dad thought it'd be a better school for them.

Willie was so smart, the teacher let her sit and "observe," they called it, in the stock market once a week. It was a class full of brainy nerds. Willie was only in third grade, but they even let her pretend she had some stocks of her own in the fifth-grade stock market.

Their school was BCS, Bethune Cookman

School, an alternative public school, called a magnet. Kids came to it from all over the city.

Bluish.

Like lightning. Came to Dreenie; and swiftly, *Bluish* was gone.

Her pal, Tuli, said Bethune was full of arty-darty kids, quick at everything.

Dreenie half admired and was half jealous of them. She would admit that much. There were other, normal kinds of kids. But Tuli tried to be arty-darty, and she tried sometimes to be Spanish, too. She often said funny stuff, like, "Ho-ney, I kid you non." Dreenie frowned, thinking about it. And, "El Esbanish, y Dominicanish, y Newyo-ricanish are muy cool."

"Tulifoolie," Dreenie called her, sometimes. Tuli knew some Spanish words, and probably got a lot of them wrong!

One time when Tuli had been mamboing down the hall between classes singing, "Chica-chica, chica-chica, do the mambo," and acting older, a girl had said something to her in Spanish.

Tuli had asked, "What?" before she thought to say it in Spanish, "Qué?"

The girl had stared at Tuli. "You give Spanish kids a bad name," she said in English. Then the girl had walked away. Dreenie had heard her.

Tuli had just stood there, Dreenie remembered. All at once, she'd burst into tears.

Dreenie hadn't known what to say. Tuli acted like she knew it all, and no one would've guessed she'd cry. But she did. Finally, Dreenie led Tuli by the arm into the girls' restroom.

"I'm nobody!" Tuli had moaned. And then, roughly, to Dreenie, "Get outta my sight, muchacha!" She was still crying hard.

Dreenie had left her there. She didn't want to get in trouble, too. "Never be where you're not supposed to be" was a school rule. But she'd wished Tuli would stop saying the Spanish words. It was dumb-acting, the way Tuli wanted to be something she wasn't. And Tuli had stayed until somebody had told a teacher she was there. Sitting all sad and alone on the floor of the girls' restroom. Tulifoolie.

At Bethune, you always got found, Dreenie thought, as prickles of snow hit her in the face. Bethune had special classes for girls who lived in a residence just for them near the school. They were the lost and found, her dad said. Tuli said she was going to live there when she was big. "Ho-ney, better than where I live ahora," was what she said. Ahora—now—Tuli lived with her granmom Gilla most of the time. With an aunt sometimes.

And no other school had Willie, who was a pest for sure. Probably a genius, too.

Dreenie marched them along the avenue, worrying that she, herself, was a dumbbell. Thinking, *Dad says some girls just show smarts quicker than others. Telling me, "You are as good as it gets—even better!" But what if it's not true?* Dreenie thought. *What if he's wrong?*

Getting ready to feel—down! All the time having to watch out for Willie, until Mommy gets home. *Six-thirty,* Dreenie thought. Mommy out in the night. Afraid sometimes something'll happen to Mommy. This big city!

It was a long time to wait. Dreenie knew that she wouldn't feel like doing homework. And no TV until the homework was done. She didn't dare turn it on or Willie would tell. She felt down, like she'd lost her puppy or something. Saw herself hugging a little pooch, and watched it disappear. Only she didn't own a puppy. She wished she did. She sure wanted one. She thought, *If I lost a puppy, it'd feel the way I do now.*

Bluish.

All the time in Dreenie's head. Fit her mood. This girl.

Through all the street noise, worrying about Willie, her shadow.

Bluish.

This girl and her dog, Lucky.

If a girl was blind, she could bring a dog to school. But no one was blind in their school, not even Bluish. This girl's puppy wasn't any Seeing Eye dog, either. Might-could be the girl was just spoiled, put-on.

Bluish. Moonlight.

Like, you see moonlight in the city? *Yeah, sure. As if!* But you can lean out the window and see the moon once in a while. Bluish moon. You see it in movies. Haven't seen anything quite her shade of pale.

"Ain't you hungry?" Willie said suddenly, shoving into Dreenie so she would slow down and talk to her. Dreenie knew all her tricks. "Can't we have some hot chocolate?"

"I'll make you some when we get home," Dreenie told her. Their mom didn't like them fooling around on Amsterdam when school was out.

"I'm not talking about the kind you make. I'm talking about good hot chocolate."

Dreenie didn't even give her sister a look. She was watching the avenue. And thinking, *Pale moonlight. Scary Bluish.*

How many times has this girl been to class since I started at Bethune? I've seen her with her puppy a few times. And then without her puppy. I want to hold her puppy! She'd seen Bluish outside after school. The bus with the lift had taken her and the puppy away.

Bitter, damp cold swept over them as Dreenie and Willie rushed along. There were deep, slushy pools at the curbs. They had to be careful, or the cars would spray it up on the sidewalk and all over them. Taking forever to get home!

"Swear to goodness, I wouldn't drive in this mess if you paid me!" she said to Willie.

"Can't *even* drive!" Willie laughed. "Ha-ha, you ain't even old enough! It ain't even really snowing yet, though," Willie added.

"What do you call this mess in my face, then?" Dreenie asked. "And will you quit it with the *ain't* stuff? It sounds so dumb."

"*Ain't* is a word, so why not use it?" Willie said, triumphantly.

"It didn't used to be, until some dumb dictionary put it in it."

"Zounds, that's messed up! 'Dictionary, put it in it.'" Willie snickered. "Dictionaries don't put words in it. People do."

"You better shut up, or I'll hex you!" Dreenie warned.

At once, Willie stopped. Her mouth turned down.

Scaring her little sister. It served her right. Willie's talking drove her crazy. She had Willie believing she could put a magic spell on her.

"Here's something you don't know," Willie said, getting her courage back. "The word *hexagram*. It's a six-sided star the Pennsylvania Dutch painted on their barns. You know why? To ward off bad vibes. But now it's just decoration. Sometimes called a hex sign."

"Will you quit?" Dreenie yelled. "I do not care to hear it!"

Willie thought she was so smart. She turned out dictionary stuff without even looking it up. Just from memory.

"I'm going to tell. You're being mean to me again." Willie began to whine. "Mommy'll give you kitchen duty for a week."

Just once, Willie had gotten the nerve to tell on her. Dreenie did get extra kitchen duty for a week. So then Dreenie had held her breath so long, her eyes bugged out and her face turned purple. Scared Willie half to death. But that was the only time.

There were kids in school who could take a million deep breaths and then fall to the floor. But to do that, you had to have friends there to catch you, ease you down. And Dreenie was still new in school. She didn't have a lot of friends. Well, maybe she had one. And she knew that any minute her so-called new best friend might catch up with them. Dreenie braced herself.

CHAPTER TWO

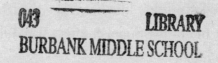

You could hear Tuli coming a block away. Singing. Sounded like, "Chica-chica, chica-chica, boom-may, bahm-ba!" Over and over. Coming at Dreenie's back.

"Chica-chica-chica!" Screams, and Tuli, Tuli-sound, in the midst of all the street noise, cars, trucks, and horns. "Mira, ho-ney, I eh-saw you looking at you-know-who! You better *be*-have yourself, or I'll tell your mah-me!" Herself a holiday decoration, laughing and getting the boys to look at her.

Some kids didn't like her. They thought she was making fun of the Spanish kids. And Tuli liked to act older, too.

Most of the girls liked her hair—brown with lighter streaks, long over her shoulders and bright in the dull day. Just the springiest curls, and she swung them from side to side as she walked, for all to see. They were like her own private jingle bells.

Tulifoolie. A year and a half older than Dreenie but in the same fifth grade.

Tuli never stopped jumping, shoving, hugging, running, talking. And most of the kids enjoyed her bopping sillies.

"Chica-chica, chica-chica, I see you, Joey! Oh, you got a girlfren'! A little chica-chica-dee tole me. Don't you lie!"

And Tuli screaming, screaming, chased by Joey as he yelled, "Girl, I'm goin' get you good!"

"Tuli, you better quit it!" someone'd yelled. Tuli this and Tuli that, up and down the avenue—Dreenie could hear them close behind her now.

"Tuli! Where'd you get the ankle boots, Tuli?"

"Ho-ney, I got frens, I got my ways—y mucho mas, splendido, girlfren'!" Chica-chica-chica. Eleven years old, but acting like a teenager.

Dreenie and Willie were at the intersection.

"Watch out, Willie," Dreenie warned her sister. "There might be ice under the slush." But Dreenie never got a chance to tell Willie to watch out for Tuli.

"Hooo!" Tuli was there. "I'm right wit you, chiquita, Willie! WILL-EEE!" Tuli slid by them. "HEY…!" She was yelling at the top of her lungs, "HELP, WILL—I AM GO…ING!" And she went sailing off the curb into the crosswalk.

Tuli hit the slush below the curb with both feet. She made a big splash all over Dreenie's coat. Unable to move, Dreenie stood there, looking down at the mess Tuli had made. She felt the wet slide down her coat and onto her tights.

Seconds later, Tuli slipped, and her feet flew out from under her. "Ahhhh!" she cried out. "Ohhhh, my tailbone!" She lay flat on her back in the middle of the intersection. Her books were still clutched in her arms. A few loose papers sailed through the icy air and settled down on top of her.

"Oh, girl! Tuli!" Dreenie cried. She and Willie ran to her.

Tuli stared up at the bleak, after-school sky.

Trying to figure if she should cry or show off, Dreenie thought.

"Get up, girl," Dreenie said. "Come on, are you hurt? We'll go to my house."

Tuli grinned. She loved going to Dreenie's house. *She must not've been hurt,* Dreenie thought.

"You look very comfortable there, darlin'. You taking a rest?" It was a crossing-guard woman, walking over to them.

Sheepishly, Tuli grinned.

"Come on, Tuli, shoot!" Dreenie said.

"Young lady, the light is going to change any minute. If you're okay, get up," the guard told Tuli. She glanced at the light, gave Tuli the once-over.

"I think I'm okay," Tuli said easily, getting up. And to Dreenie, "I coulda been hurt. You don't care! I was looking for you guys up ahead, an'en, there you were!" She was steady on her feet now. "I'm all wet," she said, looking into Dreenie's eyes.

Now I'll have to take care of her, too, Dreenie was thinking. "Come on," she said. "Take your books. I'm not carrying them."

"Okay," Tuli said. She looked all disheveled but happy.

"Wow, Tuli, that was a good one!" Willie said.

"Gracias, for inviting me over," Tuli said shyly, to Willie. "Thanks, Dreenie."

Not exactly inviting you, Dreenie thought, but she didn't say it. "Come on," she told Tuli. "You hold on to Willie for a while."

"Ain't nobody needs to hold on to me!" Willie said. But she liked Tuli. Tuli was older and paid attention to her.

"Come on, chiquita, you don't want to fall like me, eh? Bueno, then. Hold on to my arm, I'll hold my books."

They went home that way, with Dreenie just ahead of them, glancing back often and telling them to be careful.

"Hokay, ho-ney, we take care. Cuidado!"

"Tuli, shut up," Dreenie said. Thinking, *It does sound like she's making fun of Spanish people. Why can't she be herself?*

They turned off of Amsterdam, going west on the street where Dreenie's family lived. Dreenie's building didn't have anything fancy, like a uniformed doorman. It had Mr. Palmer, who stood at the door from the time school was out to 10:00 P.M., when the grown-ups were home. Sometimes Mr. Palmer opened the door for people if they had groceries or were older.

The building had double outer doors and a large space before the inner locked doors. Dreenie had her key, always on a cord around her neck. Willie had an extra one in a plastic envelope taped to the inside bottom of her lunch box. In case Dreenie's got lost somehow. It never had.

Mr. Palmer watched as Dreenie unlocked the door.

"Whyn't he ever open it for yous?" Tuli muttered.

"We're supposed to open it with our own keys," Willie said.

Dreenie said nothing.

Mr. Palmer held the door open for them once she'd unlocked it. "Student ladies," he said.

"Hi, Mr. Palmer," both Dreenie and Willie said. They felt the warmth from the radiators and were happy to be inside.

Tuli was looking around at everything in the

lobby, the way she always did. When they were in the elevator, she said, "Can't get over it. They put that little Christmas tree and lights and stuff right on that pretty table. And with pretty presents all under the tree? And nobody takes nothing? Ho-ney, hush!"

"Those packages are just for decoration," Dreenie told her. "They're empty boxes."

They went up to the third floor. Dreenie had her key ready. At number 3F, she unlocked the door and let them in. Once inside, she led them to the room she shared with Willie.

"So nice!" Tuli said to them. "You get to have your own room." Tuli always said this when she came to Dreenie's apartment.

Someday, to have her very own room by herself, and in their own house, was another one of Dreenie's most secret wishes.

"Take off those wet clothes before you sit, Tuli. You can leave on your sweater," Dreenie said. "I'll put them in the dryer so you can wear them home." She took out some pajama bottoms for Tuli to wear.

"I can put my things in the dryer," Tuli said.

"Just…entertain Willie."

"Yeah!" said Willie. "Entertain me with some food!"

"I can make her something," Tuli called. Dreenie knew Tuli would love to get into the things in the kitchen.

"What can I have to eat?" Willie whined. "I'm starving, Drain!"

"Don't call me that! You wait," Dreenie hollered back, on her way to the dryer. "I'll get to you in a minute."

"Me, too?" Tuli called.

Sometimes the two of them made her sick. "In a minute!" she called. *I'm only ten,* Dreenie thought.

She went to a hall closet where they had a built-in washer and dryer stacked one above the other. She put Tuli's clothes in the dryer and took off her coat. She did nothing about the damp tights she had on. They would dry on her.

Next, in the kitchen, she found potato chips. *Good,* she thought. *That'll make 'em happy for a minute.* She made chocolate milk and heated it. And made sandwiches. Poured the milk into glasses. Put napkins under her arm and carried a bag of chips in her left hand. Called for Tuli. "Get the hot chocolate I made for you guys."

Tuli ran to the kitchen to get it.

"Sit on the floor," Dreenie told them, back in her room. "And be careful, don't spill anything." They listened to her and were careful. No smart-mouth from Willie, either. "Chocolate, I love it!" Willie said. "Umm, umm, umm."

Dreenie got herself some orange juice. She sat back down on the space they'd made for her. Tuli was on one side of her and Willie on the other. She let herself melt down in comfort. Eased her shoulders into a comfortable sag.

Just the three of them. Silence and calm were streaming through the windows into them. And now she could take a first deep breath.

Dreenie saw when Tuli's face relaxed into quiet. She didn't have to cover up anything with the sillies. What was it? Being lonely? No mom at home?

Covering up how she feels with noise and *chica-chica-ing* all the time?

Dreenie tried to never let herself think unhappy thoughts. She held herself in. But it was kind of hard coming home each day to an empty place. All day, not knowing what was going on with your mom or dad. And it was hard to go to a new school. Tuli had been the first kid to be nice to Dreenie, to become her friend.

Noises of the day, buses, cars, people, seeped into the room. *Sounds of my city,* Dreenie thought. She loved New York. Every kid she knew loved New York. It scared them sometimes. But now, in their slow time of enjoying a snack, the city sounds didn't upset them.

Tuli watched, doing exactly as Dreenie and Willie did. Take a bite. Put the sandwich down. Wipe your mouth. Take a sip of hot chocolate.

How many times had she brought Tuli home with her? *Not for any special thing,* Dreenie thought, *but because Tuli didn't want to go to her own home.*

Dreenie was pretty sure Tuli had "staged" her

slide into the slush. She probably hadn't meant to fall down. Still, she'd done what Dreenie and her mom called a "Tuligram." It was a message telling them that Tuli needed to be someplace, with somebody in a normal life for a little while.

"Am I staying for supper?" Tuli asked, finally.

Willie knew to be quiet.

"No, Tuli," Dreenie said. "Your granmom Gilla will be looking for you."

Sometimes they let Tuli stay. But today, Dreenie didn't feel like it.

"I can call her. She'll want me to stay."

"She'll want you home before dark. And anyway...you know how soon it gets dark now," Dreenie said. "Winter."

"But I promised Willie I'd read to her," Tuli pleaded. She looked at Willie, didn't dare look at Dreenie. Willie kept her eyes on the potato chips.

"Tuli..." Dreenie began, and stopped. She knew it was Willie who read to Tuli. Willie could read a lot better than even Dreenie could. Willie never stumbled over words or was stumped by them as

Tuli was. Tuli would take up the book and start out. But then, all eager, Willie would take the book out of her hands. "You can read for fifteen, twenty minutes, but then you have to go."

"Call my granmom—"

"Take it or leave it, Tuli," Dreenie said. "And I'm not being mean. I'm really not."

Maybe I am, she thought. She sighed and finished her food. Then she carried the plates and glasses into the kitchen. Dreenie stood a moment at the sink, cleaning up. She could hear Willie and Tuli in the bedroom, laughing about something. *I'd love to have some girl as a friend. Not like Tuli. But a girl I could talk things over with. Do special things with,* Dreenie thought. Having Tuli around was like having a slower Willie. Yet she was Dreenie's only close friend. And why?

JOURNAL

***

Bluish: Time Passes. She Comes And Goes.

I never know when she's going to be there in class. When she is, she'll move her chair to a study table or by the teacher.

I figure some days she's friendlier than others. Some kids say she's not feeling well. Other kids don't seem to care about her.

Jamal tried to snatch her hat. Bluish made this bad noise in her throat. I thought she was choking. She vomited. It smelled bad! In class, in front of everybody. Ms. Baker took Bluish out and went to get a custodian. The kids went: E-ew! E-ew!

Me and Tuli and Max the aide put paper towels over it. Made me feel sick.

When Ms. Baker was gone, the kids got raucous. When they get rowdy they listen to me telling them to quit it, even though I haven't been in school that long—because I'm the biggest girl. Mommy says it's not my size, but that I have the way of a leader. So I told all of them to shut up and sit down. And most did!

"Who needs a vomiting kid in class?" Dassan said.

I said, "Shut up, Dassan."

"Girl, you can't tell me what to do," he said.

"She just did!" Jamal said. Everybody laughed. I think Jamal likes me. E-ew!! But this is not about me. It's about Bluish.

She's way tired all the time. I sit next to her when we do writing. She can write okay. But mostly she does her Game Boy. Lario. And some other kind of little man—Poke'red something. Willie plays a Game Boy sometimes. But Bluish can punch it up really fast. Then she'll drop it all of a sudden. Not even look at me.

I can't help watching her. She's so pale blue.

And she scared me. She said, "You wanna play?"

I said—I almost stuttered—"Sh-h-hure!"

I was going to take up the Game Boy when she said, "You can come over. My mom'll come get us."

I liked to died. I thought she was asking me to play with the Game Boy. But she meant playing at her house?

What if I catch something from her? I couldn't move, didn't look at her.

She made this funny sound. Then: "Stupid dork-head." She said it under her breath. But I heard her. Talking about me.

I didn't know what to do. I felt bad. Afraid of her. I felt stupid. What is wrong with me? It dawns on me maybe I really am dumb!

And she wanted me to come home with her.

She could've been my friend.

CHAPTER THREE

Dreenie didn't want to hurry. She just wanted to take her time telling her mom about it. She didn't want to tell it all at once.

Natalie. Cool Bluish.

"Dreenie, if you have something to tell me, then tell me, don't fool around."

"Make Willie stop calling me Drain! She does it all the time!"

"Is that it? Arguing with your little sister?"

"No."

"If you have something to tell me…" her mom said again.

"Guess you're tired," Dreenie said. "S'why you're short with me."

Bluish. I hate her, Dreenie thought. *Scary sickness, and I was afraid it'd rub off on me. Maybe she can still be my friend, but I don't know how. All the moonglow.*

Her mom paused to give her a look. Made Dreenie laugh nervously.

"Dreen-boat, I'm not being short with you. But, changing the subject," her mom said, "you can set the table before your dad gets home. Dinner will be ready after that."

So Dreenie just started in. Bluish. Her little puppy.

Dreenie spoke carefully to her mom while her mom made dinner. Just the two of them in the small, neat kitchen.

"She's the only one in school with a wheelchair," Dreenie told her mom.

And she described how this girl stood out, or sat out. Outside, after school, in her wheelchair. Bluish sat there in the gray while it snowed big flakes, beautiful, like Christmas. Snow on her ski jacket. Bluish had on pink mittens. Wore a pink fuzzy hat.

"And so?" her mom asked.

Dreenie felt funny inside. She almost couldn't get the words out. She calmed herself. Then she took a deep breath and let it out. "Mom? It was like a cloudy day, and seeing her? Moonglow is what...what she reminds me of. And...and...scary-looking? And in a pink hat and pink mittens? Her jacket was fuchsia color. And she is so pale!"

"Well, for heaven's sake, Dreenie." Her mom's expression showed she could see the Bluish child, and was caring about her.

"Mommy! And she's got no eyebrows, either. Her veins show through her face, all skinny trails. Picture this, Mommy. She's got no hair. Kids say she's way bald! So she wears these funny caps or hats down over her head."

Her mom looked thoughtfully at her. "Well, then, she's sick, Dreenie. I mean, bald, her hair is falling out, or already fell out."

Bluish?

"Maybe a childhood leukemia. You know? It happens," her mom said. "She's in school, so she must be better," her mom said. "She lost her hair from the strong chemotherapy, I suspect. Likely, her hair will grow back."

Dreenie sat for a long time, looking at her mom. "What if it won't grow back?" she finally thought to say. "Wow, wouldn't that be so gross." And thought, *Bluish wanted me to go home with her!*

"It probably will grow back," her mom assured her.

"I don't want to talk about her anymore," Dreenie said. A kid with—cancer!

"Being really sick is no fun for any child, Dreenboat. And you mustn't be afraid of her because she looks different. You could be nice to her—what's her name? I mean, treat her like you would treat any other school friend."

Smirking, Dreenie said, "I saw this little third-grade kid, just like Willie? Going down the hall. And he ups and bites another kid. No kidding! Mr. Darcy saw what happened. The bitten kid was screaming and crying. Man, did that biter kid get it!"

"Okay," her mom said. "You don't want to talk about the girl anymore."

"I don't care anything about her. Why should I?"

"Dreen…"

Scary Bluish.

"Just because she's in a wheelchair—Dreenie, don't single her out because of it."

"I didn't!" Dreenie said. She was already on to something else. "Mommy, Tuli always wants to stay for supper."

"Well, let her."

"No! It means that her granmom Gilla won't get to eat until later. Tuli has to fix food for her granmom! She gets on my nerves sometimes. I get tired of worrying about her."

"Oh, Dreenie. You sound so old. She just wants to be around a family."

"But it's *my* family. And I want it to myself!" She pouted until she had to laugh at herself.

Her mom laughed, too. "Set the table for me, babe," her mom said.

"Can I go down and wait for Dad?"

Her mom looked at the clock. "It's dark out."

"It's not dark in the lobby. And Mr. Palmer is there."

"Then stay inside the locked doors with Mr. Palmer. Don't go out in the street."

"I won't. It's too cold."

"Set the table, then go down."

"Where's she going?" Willie yelled, coming into the kitchen.

"To the moon, baby chile," Dreenie said. "You can't come. Set the table."

"Dreenie," her mom said.

"I'll be glad when she grows up," Willie told her mom.

"I'll be glad when *you* grow up!" Dreenie said back.

"You two! Not another word, either of you," her mom warned.

They stayed quiet. Willie took Dreenie's place when she got up to set the table. Dreenie set it in fast time. And as she left the apartment, finally, she heard her little sister tell about the nerdy stock market class, and how she loved the shapes of things, and how they changed all the time. The things that kid could think up!

Downstairs, Dreenie told Mr. Palmer, "I'm waiting on my dad again. He's always later when it's zero-cold and icy. He has to come all the way up from downtown."

Mr. Palmer nodded, didn't say anything. He looked sleepy, sitting in his chair by the locked lobby doors.

"I got my key," she told him. "I'm just going out to the front."

Mr. Palmer kept quiet. She knew it wasn't his job to look out for her.

Dreenie peered through the outer doors, up and down the street. But Mr. Palmer was to her back, and that made her feel safe. From what? *From anybody,* she thought. *Anybody with bad plans.*

People rushed by in the cold. Huddled in their coats. Newspapers, grocery bags. Getting home faster so the cold couldn't get them. She peered around and saw the lights of Broadway, all kinds of holiday lights. Made her jump up and down inside. She stepped outside for a fast minute. She looked up and down the street, but saw no one. The street was clearing of people. Winter evenings and empty streets in a city so big.

She turned back, went inside the outer doors, took out her key. Someone came in behind her. She froze. Her mind went dead, and she felt the cold.

"Dreenie."

"Daddy!" *Oooh, you scared me!*

"You're out here, and you know you shouldn't be."

"But I looked up and down, and there was no one."

"I came across the street through the parked cars. Anybody could do that, and you wouldn't see them. Remember what I told you? Look three ways when you look out the doors. Left and right and across."

"I forgot about across," she said.

"But you need to remember."

"I'll remember. I won't go out and look anymore, I promise." And she meant it.

"How's my girl?" he asked her when they went in.

"Fine, Daddy," she told him.

He spoke to Mr. Palmer a minute. About the

weather, about the New York Knicks. Basketball. Then he and Dreenie took the elevator.

Dreenie told her dad about Tuli, and about this girl who had her own chair-on-wheels.

"I like the way you put that," he said. "It makes her, well, maybe a new kind of individual."

"Yeah, that's right!" Dreenie agreed.

It surprised her how easily she could tell things to her dad. But then, she didn't tell him some things, like how she *felt* about Bluish. "Her name is Natalie," she said. "Mom says she has leukemia. Or she had it."

Her dad glanced at her. She was staring at the floor. "I bet she's better, though," he said. "She's in school."

"Guess so," she murmured. *She asked me to come home with her* was what Dreenie didn't tell him.

He put his arm around her. The elevator opened, and they went out.

"Dreen, you all right? You worried about Natalie, huh? She's your friend?"

"She threw up in class. It was gross, Daddy! I mean, e-ew! Kids just went nuts."

Scary Bluish!

"That's too bad. But anybody can get sick. The flu. It doesn't have to be…anything more than that."

"Daddy? Do…do kids get sick…and die, I mean, real easily?"

"No, not at all. Kids are tougher than anybody! Dreen, she's in school with you." And quickly, before she could tell him how scary it all was, he changed the subject. "You haven't told me what you want for Christmas."

You won't get what I want, she wanted to say.

"You and your sister, remember? You get one special present each."

"Anything?"

"Anything within reason."

"Well, what does that mean?"

Her dad laughed.

He knows what I want. What I've always wanted.

CHAPTER FOUR

The Project

Dreenie got to class just after Ms. Baker emptied her briefcase and put her lunch in her desk. "Well, good morning to you, Dreanne," Ms. Baker said, calling Dreenie by her proper name. "We're both the first ones today. I don't know what I would do if I didn't see you or Tulithia near the front of the morning!" She used Tuli's full name, also.

Grinning, "Yes, ma'am. Morning, Ms. Baker," Dreenie said.

Then Ms. Baker got busy with her work. And Dreenie went to the fake tree in the corner, on the couch side of the room, just beyond the double windows. She bent low behind the tree and was careful not to knock into any of the decorations. She found the plug and put it in the wall socket. Suddenly, tiny lights blinked: on, off, on, off, on, off, red, green, and white, over and over.

"It's magic, Ms. Baker!" Dreenie exclaimed. Straightening up, she stood still a moment to admire their tree.

All week students had been bringing in ornaments for it. There was a Santa Claus and her own shiny reindeer that Dreenie liked the best. Ms. Baker had brought a kinara, the candelabra with seven branches, for the Kwanzaa holiday. It was on a bookcase. There was a small menorah for Hanukkah on a corner table. Bluish had brought that in. It had nine candles and nine branches. They had books in the bookcase about each holiday, Christmas, and Ramadan, too. Somebody had been eating the candy canes that Ms. Baker put on the tree. "Oh, I don't mind," she said, when Dreenie told her. "It's the magic of the holiday spirit and a new year coming!" She added a few more candy canes each day.

Dreenie could hear students in the lower, then upper halls. She heard lockers banging open, click-slamming shut. And then the rush and busy murmurings as students found their places. The littlest kids were in the downstairs classes. There was the muffled sound of school buses crunching frozen slush in front of the school building.

Bluish!

Dreenie took up her book bag and leaned in on the side of the couch. She sat there, in her place, as the building rang with sounds, echoing noise. She closed her eyes a moment. She could hear that some first- and second-grade classes downstairs were having a party, first thing. She got a whiff of a warm, sweet, cookie smell, rising on the air to the top floor and this fifth-grade double room.

My new school—not new anymore! And my class. *This, my corner,* Dreenie thought, looking around. Always she thought that, first thing in the morning, claiming one corner of the couch.

She took out her yellow pad about the project they would do. They had to decide about it. She would keep notes. But she wasn't the one to write it all down. And she waited for the room to fill, warm and cozy with all the kids she knew. She had come to feel a good part of the whole. Even though she was closest to Tuli, she had no special friend yet. But she liked all her classmates. The students went to their lockers, one by one, or two by two, and then they came in. Rid of their coats. Cheeks flushed in a rosy glow.

Two weeks had passed since Dreenie had told her mom about Bluish.

If Bluish came today, she might stay for the whole day because of the project. A few times her mom had come for her when she'd had a doctor's appointment. One time, on the spur of the moment, Dreenie had asked Ms. Baker to let her and Tuli see that Bluish got to the first floor, and she'd let them.

So yesterday, when Mrs. Winburn came and waited downstairs, Dreenie and Tuli got on the elevator after Bluish. They made sure the door stayed open until her chair wheels were inside. They hung back on each side of her. She had her puppy with her, and they petted its head.

"Lucky, you get to ride, too," Dreenie had said, smiling. Looking down at the floor. Pretending she and Tuli were on the early shift for lunch. And not there just to watch out for Bluish.

Well, they didn't need to pretend. Bluish knew from the start. She'd looked up at them, in the half-minute it took to go down. Dreenie couldn't say what the look was exactly. But she'd come to know the many different ways Bluish had of looking at you. Sad looks, afraid looks, and watchful ones. One of her mean looks could just cut into you.

But yesterday, Bluish had looked pleased to have Dreenie and Tuli there. They'd reached the ground floor with Bluish. It was Dreenie's turn to take hold of her chair and push it off the elevator. One time, Bluish had said, "I can do it." Tuli had said the same thing. But Tuli would jerk the chair and scare Bluish. Sometimes, when Bluish was frightened, Lucky would bark. *Rrrr-rrrr-rrr!* it sounded like.

"You tell me when you want one of us to push you," Dreenie had told Bluish. Over a couple of weeks, there grew this way of talking and doing things between them. It blossomed and spread all over the classroom.

It was as if Dreenie knew how to act toward Bluish. Never too close, never too far away. Never to put on being friendly, but always be yourself.

"Hola, girlfren'!" It was Tuli, up right in her face.

Dreenie jumped, startled, she'd been thinking so hard. "Tuli," she said evenly.

Tuli plopped down beside her on the couch. Kids were taking their places. They knew what to do. Ms. Baker and the college intern, Max McKee, had prepared them. They were to get started on special interest projects. In some way, they were to present something unique about their city.

Max had helped them form into groups, four or five of them in a group. Dreenie, Tuli, and Paula, who came by bus, but she was allowed to take the subway sometimes. And Natalie.

Bluish! Dreenie had asked for her when none of the other groups had. Today they would spend time discussing their projects. They had more than a week to research, collect data, write, and present. Ms. Baker said each one of them had an equal share in what they decided to do. "You'll need to cooperate with one another," Ms. Baker told them, once the class had settled in. "You'll have to figure it all out, and agree about it. It would help if you would write down the agreement, just a few sentences. I'd like to see it."

Dreenie and Paula had the privilege of leaving the school grounds to walk over to Broadway. It was on file in the office that they could have lunch outside at one of three places approved by the school. Paula had thought up the project. Since they all knew Broadway, they would photograph some of what they saw every day. That would be their data. Dreenie wished she'd thought of it. All of them were eager to have it work.

Bluish came in, always last when she came at all. Almost always the first to leave. Rolling in her chair right up to the couch. They all said hi to her. She had her puppy, Lucky, in her lap. He was wearing a little knit dog coat that matched Bluish's hat.

"So cute!" Tuli exclaimed.

Bluish took Lucky's coat off, but she didn't remove her hat. It was a chartreuse-green and blue-and-red skull hat that pulled down over her ears. Dreenie thought the combination of colors made Bluish look paler, bluer.

They talked about how cold it was.

"Wish summer would hurry up," Dreenie said. She smiled at Bluish. Reached over and petted Lucky.

Bluish watched.

Then they got down to work. First, they agreed that Paula should write down everything on her yellow pad because she had the best handwriting.

"Okay, I'm ready to write the agreement," Paula said, tossing her long, black hair. "What's it to be?"

"Let's talk about who's good at what," Bluish said.

"Yeah!" Dreenie said. "Tuli's good at seeing everything on the street, and she can tell Paula a lot of things to write down."

"I know everything between here and 113th Street," Tuli told them. "I kid you non!"

"Knows everything and everybody. I've seen her," Dreenie said, matter-of-factly.

"Who could miss her?" Paula said dryly, writing it down. "Okay. Then what will you do?" she asked Dreenie.

"I can take the pictures. I've used my dad's camera before. It's a good one."

She was about to ask Paula to be her backup when Bluish said, "I can help you."

"Really?" Dreenie asked.

"I'm allowed to go outside," she said in her squeaky voice. It seemed to come from deep inside of her. "Just so long as there's somebody responsible with me."

Surprised, they couldn't help staring at her. *Pale little thing in a wheelchair,* Dreenie thought. *Well, why not?*

"We'll have to take turns pushing you, then," Paula said. "I don't think I'll be any good at that." She fidgeted, looking away as Bluish smirked at her.

"It's not anything hard to do," Dreenie said. They fell silent a moment, surrounded by the noise of other students talking, asking Ms. Baker and Max questions.

"We need to figure out how it should happen from point to point," Bluish said. Her bony hands roamed over Lucky's sleek fur. Her voice seemed larger as each day they grew more used to the sound of it.

Dreenie, Bluish, and Paula were quick to understand the process. Quick to realize that they had to show Tuli. "Here's what we're doing, Tuli. You remember?" Dreenie asked.

"I forget."

"We're going to go out of school maybe on Wednesday and look around. We'll all go together and take some pictures, too."

"So what's the agreement?" Paula asked. "What am I writing down to show Ms. Baker?"

"Let's just write, 'Ours is a street project,'" Bluish said. "'There will be photographs and word descriptions of Broadway on a poster board mounting.'"

"Hey, that's really good!" Paula said. "I'll write it, okay? Agree, everybody!" They all agreed.

"Sign it with all our names," Dreenie said.

"Put mine first," Tuli said.

"Tuli, let's do it alphabetically," Dreenie said. "D, first. Then N, for Natalie. Then Paula, then Tuli."

"Putting me last," Tuli said. "Thank you very much, my homey!"

"Well, somebody has to be last," Paula said. "That's nothing."

"Somebody has to be first and second," Bluish said, with a faint smile. "I've never been first at anything!" She managed a short, squeaky laugh. They grinned, and then they laughed.

After they'd made a general plan, they could choose the size of the poster board and where they would put it. "We'll take lots of pictures," Dreenie said. "Won't we, Bluish?"

Bluish frowned. "My mom doesn't like kids calling me that. But you can. It depends on the spelling."

Dreenie didn't understand. "Sorry! Natalie, then." She felt embarassed.

"Forget it," Bluish said.

It hadn't taken them long to plan their project. Max read their agreement and gave it an okay.

Afterward, Bluish wheeled up to one of the big tables, with Lucky on the floor beside her. He looked up at her eagerly and jumped around whenever a kid got up. But he didn't stray far from Bluish's side. She gave him tidbits. And he had a little bone he chewed on.

Bluish cut paper and made a sign. Rolled over to the decorated tree and taped the sign to one of the branches. It read *Hanukkah Bush* in black marker. Ms. Baker watched Bluish but made no comment. Kids like Dreenie, who saw Bluish go up to the tree, didn't say anything, either.

Bluish made a second sign. She wound string around two paper clips. She clipped them to the sign and put the sign around her neck. The letters were squiggly, not as bold as on the other sign. *I was born human. I'm named Natalie.*

Underneath that were tiny printed words: *But you can call me Blueish.*

Dreenie braced herself when Bluish came toward her. Bluish struggled now to turn the wheels. "That's what you mean, right?" Panting, she said to Dreenie, "'Cause of my coloring." She pointed to the sign's tiny letters.

"I'd take the *e* out," Dreenie said. "It's Bluish, without the *e*."

"Oh, okay," Bluish said. "You fix it."

Dreenie got a marker and crossed out the *e*. "There. B-l-u-i-s-h."

"Okay." Said barely above a whisper.

We've gotten used to her—sort of, Dreenie was thinking. *Each day with her around is different. Sometimes good, sometimes bad. What a freaky kid! You can tell she's been sick bad, maybe a long time. And you can't help feeling sorry for her.*

Still, Bluish was like nothing Dreenie had ever seen. When she got an upset stomach, as she sometimes did, Dreenie didn't want to be around her. Every kid got anxious when it happened. Some kids

said there was an odor around her and her chair—
like medicine. One time, a kid said, "Hey, girl, you
smell like the clinic."

And Bluish said right back, "Airhead! Your
pea-brain's crawling out the door!" The kid—it
had been Kevin Smith—didn't know what to make
of her. Most kids didn't. She always had something peculiar to say back when a kid was nosy or
dumb-acting.

About a half-hour before lunch, Tuli had gotten
bored and was *chica-chica-ing* up and down the
room. She stopped by Bluish, who was reading a
book from the bookcase. "What's them things
you got there in your lap next to the doggie?"
she asked.

Bluish answered, "You want one?"

"One what?"

"They're fitted hats to come down low on your
head," Bluish said. "It's what I wear."

"Why?" Tuli asked.

"'Cause, that's why." Bluish sounded hoarse.
She had talked more today than usual, Dreenie
realized.

Bluish handed Tuli a hat out of a small plastic bag.

"Oooh!" Tuli said, and she put it on. The hat was knitted in blue and gold, with a purple background. "I got too much hair!"

"No, you don't," Bluish told her. Her little voice squeaked almost to losing it.

She took another hat from the plastic bag and held it out to Dreenie.

"Really? I get to wear it?" Dreenie asked.

"I made it for you. You can have it."

Dreenie couldn't believe it. "That's so nice!" she said. "Thank you!"

They were talking quietly, not to cause too much attention. But other kids saw and came over and hung around like they wanted a hat, too. Until Max asked if they had finished their work.

Bluish watched in the frowning way she had as Dreenie tried on her hat. Dreenie thought it was beautiful, the prettiest one of all. It had a gold background. It had a red stripe and a spring-green one. "It looks like Christmas!" Dreenie said. She stuffed her hair under and pulled the hat low over her ears.

Bluish nodded okay.

There was a mirror on the closet door. Dreenie and Tuli looked at themselves.

"I got too much hair," Tuli said. "It don't look right on me." But she was admiring herself.

"You don't have to put all that hair under it," Dreenie told her. "Just let it out. Bluish wants us to wear them," she whispered.

"Okay, I get it," Tuli whispered back. "But it don't look right on me!"

In the mirror, Bluish was there with them. She'd come up from behind. Dreenie laughed; she hadn't expected to see her. Dreenie and Tuli stood still, looking at themselves, at the hats, and Bluish in her hat.

"We look way cool!" Bluish murmured.

Tuli pulled her hair down from under the hat. Her curls sprang around, as if they had a life of their own. "I am the baddest, I kid you non!" Tuli said.

She is the silliest, no doubt about it, Dreenie thought. It was then that she realized Bluish was standing, the same as they were. "Bluish!" Dreenie exclaimed.

Something bright and alive suddenly drained from Bluish's eyes. She turned away. That quickly, her mood had changed.

She took a paperback off the bookshelf; a minute later, she shakily put it back. She was hobbling now, as if her legs wouldn't hold her up. She went over to study the big dictionary, which was always in place at the end of one of the tables. When she got up five minutes later, it took her a long time. She made her way to her chair, holding onto things. There she rested, with Lucky in her lap. Turned in the chair, looking for Ms. Baker.

There were strings of saliva hanging out of her mouth. Ms. Baker saw her. Came to her. "Call my mom," Bluish whispered. "Please."

Ms. Baker gave her tissues for her mouth. Then she said something to Max, and he left the room. Bluish closed her eyes, held the tissues to her lips.

"Go about your business," Ms. Baker told them.

Then Bluish fell asleep.

The class made more noise shushing one another than if they'd just stayed quiet. That was what Ms. Baker told them.

Max came back and wheeled Bluish away.

Bluish: What Bluish Had To Say

A few days later.

See, Bluish musta told Ms. Baker.

"Class. Natalie has something to tell you," Ms. Baker said. And Bluish said, "Now don't get me wrong. But me and my mom made some hats. See, I had to stay in bed when I got real sick way before? And then I found out I could do things with my hands." Bluish all the time has to stop, take a breath. "So since I've been home, we finished making knit hats for everybody here. My mom helped me."

Can you believe it? Every kid smiled at her.

And walked up to her, to give her five. You move your hand slow at Bluish. You don't jerk fast, because she can't get out of the way and you might hurt her.

Kids gave her a low five fingers. Kids said, "You didn't have to. That's a lot of work. I didn't bring anything for you." And Bluish said, "I already did it. I don't want anything!"

And each kid got one. Bluish said, "Here Jody," to Ms. Baker. A lot of kids call the teachers by their first names. In my other school where I went, we didn't. So I call her Ms. Baker.

Everybody held their hats. Kids didn't want to look foolish.

Bluish said, "Well, they're yours. You can wear 'em when you want."

And kids saying Bluish's name, "Bluish, Bluish." Well, that's what we call her.

At Bluish's

Bluish's mom—I don't think she likes me. But I

went to her house, Bluish. Me and Tuli and Willie. Why come? Because Bluish said we could, too.

So funny, my bratty sister. Crawled up on the bed. They had Game Boys, but Willie put her thumb in her mouth, curled up by Bluish in her bed, and went to sleep. Bluish looked at Willie like she was a doll-baby. Bluish's little mouth gave a grin.

I felt so good, I knew Bluish wanted us to be there. Tuli sat on a chair. Couldn't sit still and had to touch everything in the bedroom.

Real nice place over on West End, near 103rd Street. None of us was scared anymore. She lives in this apartment called a classic eight. Eight rooms! Big as a house! I loved it. And Lucky the dog has a little bed on the floor in Bluish's room! Little black fur legs running, barking its little dog bark. So cute. Oh, I wish…

We were sorting pictures of Broadway. Her mom had said it was too cold for Bluish that Wednesday when we went out for our project. Willie had said, "Shoot, we could have helped Bluish have some fun." So I had to take all the pictures without her. My dad's camera. Tuli showed us stuff.

I know stuff about our 'hood, but Paula doesn't. She's from Brooklyn. But Tuli just sees stuff that I miss. She found this place? It was an Irish bar and a Chinese restaurant. Not too big but with maybe six booths for eating egg rolls and stuff. Cool! Called Misters Side by Side, with a green four-leaf clover and Chinese writing. How'd I miss it?

We only looked in. Then I took its picture—the yellow door and red letter sign. Tucked in there between a butcher's and a cleaner's. I took them too. I never even saw it. Maybe Misters Side by Side only just got there.

We got the film developed in a day. An evening later, Bluish called and said to bring the pictures over, she might be out the next day. So we did.

We get there, and I spread all the pictures on top of asleep Willie. And real easy, Bluish reached one to look at.

Paula couldn't come. Said it would be okay, whatever we picked. But if there was one she loved, we'd have to use it. Said she loved Lightly Shoes. Barzinis. And Jays Fishes.

Bluish—her mom. She is Rita Winburn. Bluish's mom comes in and we stare at her and wait. Somehow we blurt our names. She has brought out little cakes and milk.

Tuli says, "Ooooh." Nice. We eat the cakes. I wake Willie.

Bluish's mom is standing at the door with her arms crossed. Bluish kind of folds the bed covers up to her chin. She eats nothing.

Her mom has dark hair and creamy skin. She is not brown. I've seen Bluish's dad. Mr. Winburn is brown. I'm sorta sweet chocolate color. Tuli is more honey color. Bluish would probably be the combined creamy and brown—her mom and dad—if she wasn't sick. But she is this ill color not like anybody.

She's Bluish because I saw her and she made me think of moonlight. But she might get creamier. Get rid of the blue someday. I hope so.

"We can hope and pray," Tuli once said.

Bluish's mom is standing there. And then her mom says, "Don't call her Blewish. That's not nice. That is derogatory."

I stood up. I must have shook my head.

"Don't you know it is not nice?" her mom asked. "Would you like her to call you bad names?" Looking right at me.

Tuli was standing, staring at the mom and then at me.

Bluish peeked through her fingers. "That's not it, Mummy," Bluish said. "I know what you are thinking and you are wrong."

Tuli waited for me to say, but I couldn't. I didn't want to talk. I felt sooo bad.

And then Tuli says all fast, "You tell her mom, Dreen! Please, Missus."

And I couldn't.

And then Bluish says, "Mom, it's not black and Jewish, B-l-e-w-i-s-h, like a bad word." She spelled it out for her mom. "But because I am so pale—from the chemo—I am a somewhat bluish color, get it?" She spelled it out, "B-l-u-i-s-h, and without the *e* in the *blue*." Bluish said, "Dreenie didn't mean anything bad."

"I didn't mean…anything bad!" That's what I told the mom. I finally got it out. "I never. I wouldn't."

Bluish said, "I bet not the other kids, either. I bet only a few started it, black and Jewish."

"She's not anyone but Bluish. B-l-u-i-s-h." It was Willie. Spelling it and saying it to Bluish's mom. Willie holding her hands up because they are sticky with cake. She pipes up again, my kid sister. "She's Bluish! She's our friend!" And then grinning all over her face. Willie, my bratty sister! And made Bluish's mom laugh!

And Mrs. Winburn said, "Well, I'd feel much better if you called her Natalie."

"They do sometimes," Bluish told her mom.

And we said we did. Although not.

But I never even knew the B-l-e-w-i-s-h part. What of that? I mean, I never even thought to call her bad because she's black and Jewish. I thought the kids were saying Bluish. And what of the B-l-u-i-s-h? Well, it's like Willie said.

Bluish made me stop and look. She made me care about what was all so scary, so sad, and so hurt with her too. To me she is just Bluish child, Bluish ill serious. Bluish close with us. Someday Bluish just like us.

Maybe.

CHAPTER FIVE

It's Going to Get Fun!

One day, the first thing, Dreenie and her project group began mounting their pictures on poster board. They took turns deciding where each picture would go.

"Perfect!" Paula said.

All the students were around their boards, at tables, and on the floor.

Bluish was in school this day, with Dreenie and the others. She'd seemed the same—quiet. Weak-like. *But not better, not worse*, Dreenie thought. There were still kids who would tease her because she looked so different, in a wheelchair, and because they knew she wasn't strong. They were mostly not in their class. Not often now did the classmates pick on her so she'd come back with a strange remark. She was there, part of the class. And they knew she wasn't strong; she was someone to watch out for. They couldn't treat her just like one of them. Because she wasn't.

Dreenie was afraid Bluish would never be like the rest of them. Bluish couldn't move fast. She couldn't get rowdy. She could be so quiet. Some days, she didn't even want her puppy around, she felt so bad. And then Dreenie would look out for Lucky. Hugging the dog. Taking him out in the school yard in the cold every so often. She felt him tremble in her hands. She shivered, too.

Dreenie let the dog lick her face. *Aren't we lucky?* she thought, joking to herself and running around the playground. Loving the puppy as if he were hers.

Dreenie's group took a long time to decide where the photos would go on their board. They finally agreed and pasted them up. Then, carefully, they typed sentences on the computer about each picture. Then, they printed them out. Next, they pasted the sentences under the pictures. When the poster board was ready, they carried it to the stairs and taped it to the wall on the side of the stairway. It wasn't easy for Tuli and Dreenie to hold it upright while Paula taped it all around. Bluish watched from the top of the stairs.

"Does it look straight?" they asked her.

"No…wait. Now it does," she told them.

"There!" Dreenie said. "We're done!"

"Max, ours is done. Look at that! First thing I ever helped make. Looking good!" Tuli said. Anyone coming up to the fifth floor or down the stairs could see their work.

Other groups also hung their poster boards of photographs. Dreenie's group had titled their board THE BIG APPLE AVENUE in large, dark letters. And right below that, in bright red, it said (BROADWAY YAY!) Some other kids had done Broadway, too.

"Not as good pictures," Dreenie said, and Paula agreed.

"Ours is the best," Bluish said, then whispered, "But don't tell. It's not a competition."

They all agreed not to brag. There were no prizes for the best. They'd been taught to try not to hurt one another. It was hard, sometimes, to always be nice. Especially for Tuli. She liked to point and go, "Oooh, hooo, that's oogily!" But she did try not to boast.

They'd worked so closely together, no one remembered now who had thought of what and which part. "Truly a group effort," Bluish said, sounding like Ms. Baker.

Tuli said, "Un-huh, chicki, you are so right on!" Tuli made them laugh. Even Bluish laughed a little.

It was a good first part of the day in school. Most everybody got the job done. All the boards were hung by the end of the morning. They had a reward party. Cookies stored in the small fridge. Punch they had made in class. Ms. Baker took out sparkling pins that said *Peace* or *Love*. Every student got a pin. It caused an uproar.

"I bet you no other class got anything like them!" kids kept saying. "Ms. Baker, you are the most, man!"

They sat around the Christmas tree. Some kids had brought little gifts to school. But nobody had to. They were taught in school that the best gifts were the ones they made for one another, like cards, or little things you knit or drew. There wasn't any special time that you made things to give. You did it when you felt like it, as Bluish had. Ms. Baker always said, "A gift is a kindness of giving."

They all sat around the tree with Ms. Baker. Max, who helped her each day, told them about Hanukkah and Kwanzaa and Christmas. Kids knew about some of it. It was New York; they saw all kinds of people. They easily picked things up about one another. Max asked who had celebrated which holidays and even other ones. "It's all right if you celebrate more than one—or none," he said.

"We do Kwanzaa," Mary Beth Neele said.

"We do Christmas and Kwanzaa," Dreenie said.

Paula said, "My folks like Christmas because it's American. But my dad is from India. Our belief is Hinduism."

Students raised their hands or spoke out.

Tuli clutched her hands together, really tight.

Dreenie saw her. "Come on, Tuli," she murmured. She knew what Tuli was thinking. Something like, "I get nothing, so why celebrate anything?" Tuli could go on for fifteen minutes about what she never got. But she always got nice things. People saw to it. Tuli's aunt gave her holiday gifts. Tuli told her granmom Gilla to remind her aunt every time. Her granmom Gilla's church gave Tuli a coat every other year. And dresses that her granmom Gilla made with the help of some others of the missionary women.

A nice coat, Dreenie thought. Not exactly the flashy kind that fit the way Tuli acted up. But a good, pretty one that fit her, not too long. Tuli did try hard, even when she got things wrong or didn't understand. But there was stuff she knew about, like people along Broadway. Given enough time, Dreenie was sure Tuli could learn the names of everybody in New York City someday. *So what if she tries to be Spanish at times,* Dreenie thought. Tuli wanted to be somebody. She wanted to be friends with everybody.

Eating cookies, just sitting around. Dreenie felt relaxed. It was time.

It had been her idea to surprise Bluish. All the

kids went along, even Jamal, who could be the worst. Dreenie was to give the signal.

Everything was quiet. Suddenly, Dreenie jumped up and gave the signal. She lifted her arms above her head and shook her fingers. Kids hollered, screeched.

"Hats on!" Ms. Baker called. She took from her smock pocket the hat that Bluish had made her, and she put it on. Students pulled hats from under sweaters, from the cupboard drawers, from wherever they'd hidden them. Even when some of them didn't want to, when they believed they looked stupid, in two seconds, they all had their hats on. "Whee!" said Ms. Baker. "This room has a rainbow condition!" They laughed loudly at that.

"Wow!" Dreenie said, looking around. The hats were many colors, with one or two stripes around.

"Look at us!" Tuli said.

Kids acted up, making faces. In spite of themselves, they admired themselves in the mirror on the closet door.

"We're a field of flowers," Bluish said softly.

"We're all the same; we're different, too. Now you all look just like me." She smiled, faintly.

They looked at one another, looked at her. Nobody disagreed. Nobody laughed. One kid, Manny Kittinger—they called him Manny the K— stood there in front of Bluish. Looking dopey in his hat, but loving it, he grinned from ear to ear. He flapped his hand at Bluish, waving. Ms. Baker had to smile; she patted Manny on his hat. It was black with orange stripes.

Kids floated easily up to Bluish and circled her chair. Touched her hand. She'd grab a hand or arm, but didn't hold on. They were careful not to get rowdy or rough.

"They're cool hats, aren't they, class?" Max, the aide, said. They all agreed the hats were the flash. They went around, admiring one another, the combinations of colors and stripes.

"This whole class is the rap!" Dassan said.

"You like that?" Dreenie asked him.

He thought a moment and said, "Yeah! Sure! Nobody else in the whole school has these hats."

"Bluish made us special," Dreenie said. And got a smile out of Bluish.

It was then that Ms. Baker said, "Class, Natalie has something she wants to show you. Now, don't crowd her. Make a big half-moon around her. Okay? That's good."

When they had arranged themselves on the floor, Ms. Baker handed Bluish something painted and square. Bluish had a sack of something to one side of her, and Ms. Baker put it on her lap. Bluish hadn't brought her dog today.

Bluish took up the square object and held it in both hands. It looked like a toy top.

They all stared. Dreenie wondered what was going to happen.

"This is my mother's," Bluish said. "It once belonged to her mother, my Grandma Celia." She breathed and seemed to pull herself in. "It's very old, maybe a hundred years."

"Wow, a whole century," someone said.

"It's called a dreidel, and children play a game with it in the evenings of Hanukkah holidays."

"You're going to teach us the game," Dreenie said.

"Dreidel, dreidel, dreidel…" Mary Beth sang. "I know a dreidel song we learned in camp. But I forget the words."

They could hear Bluish humming for a moment. It was the same melody that Mary Beth had sung.

"Class, let Natalie show us the dreidel game."

"You play with peanuts or coins or sticks, but I only have enough peanuts for maybe six or seven people."

But everyone wanted to play. "You'll have to take turns. Listen up," she said.

And they listened as Bluish explained about the dreidel. "It's a four-sided top that you spin. Each side has a Hebrew letter—this side, this letter, is called *nun*." She turned the dreidel. "This side is *gimel*; this side is pronounced *hey*; and the last, it's *shin*."

They laughed at the strange sounds of the words. Someone went, "Hey-hey-hey!"

Instantly, another kid went, "Shinny-shin-shin!"

"Class, don't make fun," Ms. Baker said. They hushed.

Bluish looked slightly upset, but their joking had given her time to catch her breath.

Dreenie watched her face. She'd been lost in the give-and-take of the class. All of them, around Bluish, listening. *That couldn't have happened two weeks ago,* she thought. Bluish continued, "The letters mean more, like a miracle, but not in the game. The first seven kids get ten peanuts. Here." She motioned for Dreenie.

Surprised, Dreenie held herself very calm as she took handfuls of peanuts from the bag and chose seven kids to have them. They were all being quiet, interested.

"Now, each player put a peanut in the middle—that's the pot."

They did.

"First player, spin the dreidel."

Bluish chose Tuli. "Like this?" Tuli asked. She didn't wait for an answer. She spun the dreidel top.

They watched it spin, grinning at its whirl.

"Okay, when it stops, we see what face of the dreidel is up," Bluish said. The dreidel fell on its side.

"The letter *hey* is up. Tuli gets half of the pot," Bluish said.

"Why does she get half?" Dassan wanted to know.

"Because *hey* stands for half, get it?"

"What does *nun* stand for?" Dreenie asked.

"*Nun* stands for *nisht*, or nothing. And the player does nothing."

"Wow."

"*Gimel* stands for *gantz*, or all," Bluish told them. "And the player who gets *gimel* gets everything in the pot."

"Ooh, I want that one!" Paula said. Others agreed.

Bluish continued: "*Shin* stands for *shtel*, to put in. The one who gets *shin* has to add two peanuts to the pot."

"Uh-uh!" kids said. They didn't want that one.

"When there're no peanuts in the pot, or only one, each player puts in a peanut. And that's how you do the game," Bluish said. "When one person wins everything, the game is over."

They played the game for a while. Everyone got

to play. Shouts of *"Shin! Shin!"* And "I got *gimel*, watch out!" It was fun. When they had to stop, they all applauded. It was time to do their math.

As they opened their books, Ms. Baker told them other things about the dreidel. "There's more to it than the game," she said. She moved about the room, ready to help them if they needed it. Talking: "What does the spinning dreidel remind you of?" she asked.

"Earth!" Dreenie said.

"I was going to say that!" Mary Beth said.

"The sun," someone else said.

"That, too," Ms. Baker said. "The dreidel shows us the changing of seasons as the sun shifts. Winter, spring, summer, fall, as the earth spins on its axis."

"Neat," Dreenie said. And smiled at Bluish. But Bluish had dozed off. She'd worn herself out.

"Class," Ms. Baker said. She put a finger to her lips and spoke softly. "Remember to bring your field trip permissions on Friday. Monday we'll go to the Natural History Museum. It's our last field trip and the last few days of school until your winter vacation."

Christmas holidays. Change of seasons, Dreenie thought. *Will she still be Bluish in the spring? Wish I knew more. She looks like she hasn't one hair on her whole skin. That's one thing. And sometimes she gives this look like she's going to scream. Like she's really mad.*

"Its proper name is American Museum of Natural History," Bluish said.

They looked at her. "Hi!" Dreenie said, startled to see Bluish was awake.

"You're back with us?" Ms. Baker said, smiling. Bluish had dozed only a few minutes.

"Going to see the dinosaurs! Yeah!" Some of the kids yelled, acting up.

"Class, we're going to see an exhibit very different from dinosaurs."

Bluish muttered something. Perhaps she meant for Dreenie to hear her. Dreenie was close enough. It sounded like, "I get to go, too!"

CHAPTER SIX

ALL

It was Friday afternoon, and Bluish had gone to the doctor. They became more worried about her each time she went. Students stood around, looking at Ms. Baker. Like Dreenie, they didn't know exactly how they were feeling. It upset them when Bluish got sick. Each time she left suddenly for the doctor, they feared she wouldn't come back.

Ms. Baker could tell, and began talking to them. "Natalie's mom doesn't want you to feel sorry for Natalie," Ms. Baker told them. "She wants you to understand that Natalie's been very sick."

It was then Dreenie thought to say, "I want to know more."

Kids said, "We want to know more!"

Ms. Baker frowned, pressing her lips firmly together. She went to the blackboard. "Natalie has ALL," she said, writing it on the board, "which is Acute Lymphoblastic Leukemia. It's a serious and painful disease."

Kids left their seats. Slowly, they came up to the front; Ms. Baker was the lamplight they were drawn to like moths. Hearing her talk about Bluish made them stop and think about this worry they'd been having. And now they could show it, they could let it out.

Ms. Baker put her chalk down and reached out to them. Dreenie took her hand a moment. Tuli had Ms. Baker by the arm. Other students did the same, when Dreenie and Tuli let go. Milling around Ms. Baker, they all watched her expression. They knew every line of her face; knew every smile and stern reproach.

"Natalie still must take medicines," Ms. Baker went on. "But once she's gone through the program, she has an eighty-five to ninety percent chance of being cured. So please, her mother asks that you treat her the way *you* would want to be treated.

And try not to feel sorry for her. Class," Ms. Baker added, "I want you to know I'm proud of you, the way you've come to regard Natalie."

"But…" Dreenie began. "But what does that mean? Eighty-five to ninety percent. Where's the rest? That's not a hundred percent."

Ms. Baker spoke clearly, yet quietly. "It means that if Natalie goes from the start of her treatment through five years without a relapse, she's probably forever cured."

They stared at Ms. Baker.

"Five whole years?" Jamal said. "Wow…that's… that's long! We'll be fifteen!"

"What's a relapse?" Dassan wanted to know.

"A relapse is a restart of an illness that's been in remission—that's been halted." Ms. Baker took up the chalk and wrote *Relapse* and *Remission*.

Their questions came one after the other. "But when did…did it start?" Dreenie asked.

Ms. Baker never answered her directly. She looked around at all of them.

"Sit down, class," she told them. "We'll talk about it."

They sat down. But soon they were up out of their seats again. Ms. Baker was used to them. They needed to talk, get close, wander away, listening, and come back to the front again.

One student, Linda, was the first to comment. "I feel bad. But I feel funny, I don't know. I guess I can't help it. I feel sorry for her."

Dreenie sat and squirmed. *All of them, talking about Bluish. Was it talking behind her back? Is it like Us against Her? Us together and Her by herself? But she's the sick one! And we're not.* Dreenie had the worst feeling of being afraid. Of what, she didn't know.

Yes, I do. Of me, getting sick, she thought. Her stomach flopped a moment.

"Class," Ms. Baker said. "Does it make you uncomfortable to talk about it?"

"Yes!" several students piped up. "Yeah, it does!"

One said, "I get scared I'll catch it. I know you can't—can you?"

"No, don't worry," Ms. Baker said.

"You don't know how to act about it," a boy, Nicholas, said.

Jamal said, "You think she's going to be just like us. Only, you do something, playing, not to hurt her. Her mouth turns down. She gets all sad. And can get mean, man! Shoot, I stay away from her."

"It seems to me you all are learning about a student who is your classmate and who has been very ill," Ms. Baker said. "What else have you learned?"

"Well, Bluish doesn't like fooling-around play, that's for sure," Paula said.

Tuli said, "She told me once she di'nt want to get bruised when kids got rowdy. 'A bruise is bloodletting. I used to bleed and bleed,' she said. I kid you non! S'what she tole us, di'nt she, Dreenie?"

Dreenie nodded. It was true, and Bluish had told Dreenie even more.

Ms. Baker said, "Tulithia, Natalie was telling you that when the illness started, she didn't have tiny blood platelets. And we all have to have them. Platelets plug the blood vessels and stop the bleeding. It must have been scary—to bleed and not stop."

Dassan raised his hand. "What stopped it, then? She don't bleed now."

"Blood transfusions," Ms. Baker said. "Medicines that worked."

Tentatively, Dreenie raised her hand. They all felt she was the one closest to Bluish.

Ms. Baker, all of them, waited. Dreenie sighed and finally said, "'Chemo is like dying.' That's what Blu—I mean, Natalie, told me. She said what made her faint was this needle they put in her back into her hipbone. She said it was a long, hollow needle that drew out the bone marrow."

"E-ew!" kids murmured. "Yuckies!"

"Class," Ms. Baker said, shushing them.

Bluish had told Dreenie things in bits and pieces and not all at one time. Dreenie remembered, though. Doing their work, talking low now and then.

"That's what the cure is about," Ms. Baker said. "It's about having no sick cells inside her bones. In the marrow." She wrote on the board: *Marrow—site of blood cell reproduction.*

Dreenie nodded. "She said they often have to stick the needle way in and draw out bone marrow to look at it and check it." It was like Bluish was in her head. She could hear her. *"That's what kills you. It hurts so bad. It sucks, man! Like sucking on a straw. It sucks your insides out. It sucks out your light."* Dreenie didn't feel she should tell them. It was something just so deep of Bluish. What she did tell them was, "She said she didn't want us talking about her illness. And here we are..." Dreenie looked down at her hands.

"I can understand her not wanting that," Ms. Baker said. "I'll take the blame. I hoped you all would learn to respect what it means to be well. To be healthy, the way you are. So that you will see more clearly what Natalie must go through." She erased everything on the board.

"I got a sore throat," Manny the K said.

"Oh, Manny!" Ms. Baker said.

"Am I going to die?"

Ms. Baker looked perturbed. "Stop it now," she told him, sternly. "I'll send you to the nurse if your throat is really bad."

"It's okay!" he said, alarmed. Looking ashamed of himself.

Kids snickered. Mr. Baker said that was enough, and to get back to work.

Friday evening, after Tuli left, after Dreenie's mom and dad were home, she called Bluish. She remembered to say Bluish's name properly.

Bluish's mom answered the ring.

"Is Natalie there? It's Dreenie, from school."

"Hi, Dreenie. Wait a minute."

Dreenie held her breath. She tried to tell if Mrs. Winburn was upset with her. But she couldn't tell. Why would she be? Dreenie thought, *Don't make up stuff.*

Bluish got on the phone. "Hi," she said.

"You sound okay," Dreenie said.

"Why shouldn't I?" she answered.

"Well, you weren't in school."

"I had the doctor's."

"Yeah, I know. Ms. Baker told us." Instantly she was sorry she'd mentioned it.

There was a pause. "You all were talking about me," Bluish said.

"We were worried," Dreenie said. "Ms. Baker told us so we wouldn't worry."

"You worried about me? I mean, all of you?"

"Yeah, sure," Dreenie said.

Silence on the other end. "I'm okay," Bluish said, finally. There was a tremble in her voice.

They talked more. Dreenie told her ordinary things that happened in school. And told her that her dad and Willie had found out about a fun thing at this middle school not far from Bethune. It was an African Market. "I mean, a whole market they'll have—it's two days after Christmas. You want to go? Tuli's going with me and my dad. She doesn't have anyone to go with. Willie's going with some friends."

"Well," Bluish said, "maybe. My dad usually has to drive when I go someplace like that. I can't walk like anybody."

"I know," Dreenie said. "It's after Christmas, on the twenty-seventh."

"I'll have to ask," Bluish said.

"Are you coming to school Monday? Remember, the field trip?"

"I know. I didn't forget. Wha'dya think?"

They talked a while; then Bluish said, "Thanks for calling."

"See ya," Dreenie said. She wanted to go over,

to see how Bluish was doing over the weekend. Maybe Bluish wouldn't feel good, though, and wouldn't want her to see. She'd say no, you can't come over. So Dreenie hung up the phone without asking.

Over the weekend, Dreenie visited Tuli. Well, Tuli came and got her.

Dreenie's mom sounded cautious with them. Telling Dreenie, "Now, I want you to stay in Tuli's house, you hear, Dreenie? I don't want you walking to the grocery or to the pharmacy. It's Sunday, everybody's home from work, out and around…"

"Uh-uh, Missus," Tuli said. "Too cold. Nobody standing out or sitting playing chess and dominoes in this weather."

"The more reason to stay inside," Dreenie's mom said. "Empty streets."

Dreenie sighed. The streets were never empty. But she knew why her mom was fearful about Tuli's neighborhood. It wasn't so bad; besides, Tuli was her friend. Dreenie guessed she really was. And sometimes you had to go visit whatever kind of friend you had, at her house.

"Well, can I at least go to afternoon services with her and her granmom?"

"That's all right, you two with Gilla."

"Well, good, at last!" Dreenie said. "We get to do something."

"Dreenie," her mom said, "you guys get to do a lot."

Dreenie wore a yellow wool sweater and a gray skirt with gray tights and black boots. She wore her winter jacket, which was burnt-gold color. It was hooded and warm.

They went uptown east around the park. Tuli's building was right there, halfway in on 112th Street. The halls were only a little warmer than the outside. Dreenie could hear people in their apartments. Radios. Television. There was no one like Mr. Palmer to greet them as they came in. No Christmas tree.

They went up. "Granmom! Open up!"

"Don't you have your key?" Dreenie asked her.

"Sure, I got my key," Tuli said. "But Granmom don't like the sound of a key in the lock. Makes her nervous."

Gilla Bennett opened the door. She was in her robe and slippers. A thin, wiry woman, she looked tired.

"Hi, Granmom Gilla," Dreenie said.

"Hello, Dreenie. You look nice!"

"I see you're not dressed," Tuli said to her granmom.

"No, don't feel much like going out today," she told Tuli. "I didn't get off the job until way late. But I made you your favorite soup, baby."

Dreenie sat down at the kitchen table. Everything was neat and clean, but bare. There was not much extra in Tuli's house. The soup smelled good on the stove. Dreenie realized she was hungry.

Tuli filled bowls with potato and meat soup. Then she sprinkled grated cheese on top.

"This is really good!" Dreenie said. There was bread that Granmom had made; Dreenie had a big piece.

"Hits the spot!" Granmom said. Dreenie and Tuli both agreed it did.

Afterward, Granmom went to take a nap. And Dreenie and Tuli cleaned off the table, did the few dishes, and put them away.

"I guess we're not going to afternoon services, then," Dreenie said finally.

"We could go. But you're not supposed to go without Granmom, and I don't want to, anyway."

"All dressed up and no place to go," Dreenie said. She didn't feel disappointed, exactly.

"Well, that's just the way it is," Tuli said. "I lead a sad life." Sounding like an actress.

"No, you don't, either," Dreenie said.

"Yeah, I do. I got up and dressed, and Granmom was still asleep." Gilla worked a night shift, helping to guard a large business.

Dreenie was silent. Finally, she said, "You got Granmom. You got me and my family." Tuli stared at her, eyes blank. "And you look like a model."

That made Tuli smile broadly. "Yeah? I do?"

"Yeah, you do!" Dreenie told her. And she meant it.

They played checkers for a while. And listened

to the radio. Sitting on Tuli's bed, they painted their nails. Tuli painted hers sunlight-yellow.

"I love Christmastime," Dreenie said, "but I can't wait for summer to come."

She painted her nails a deep rose.

"We ought to make a resolution to do something different each week next summer," Tuli said.

"Maybe by then, Bluish can go do stuff with us, and walk, too."

"You're always thinking about her," Tuli whined. "What about me?"

Dreenie sighed. She let it go. But soon after, she said she had stuff to do.

She went home, relieved. Soon, she'd be seeing Willie and her mom and dad.

❦

Bluish: Trip Out In The Field, The Vivarium

Well, how could you guess? I didn't. Nobody did.

We get on the bus. And Bluish, she gets to go! She's as excited as me, only we don't show it.

"Tuli, stop jiggling!" we tell Tulifoolie and we all laugh. Then we all jiggle and the bus goes.

We had all the kids and Max and Ms. Baker. Guess what? Mrs. Winburn! She came with us. But she sat with Max, talked to him. She didn't bother us. Bluish told her mom she wouldn't speak to her if she watched us or anything. Whoop! We didn't even notice her mom after a while. But how could anyone guess, huh?

Yay! We get down there. And there! Natural History Museum. Central Park West at 79th. Really great with flags blowing in the cold. We get out—I want to count the steps with the rest of the kids. But how's Bluish going to get up so many steps?

Her mom pointed to the sign. I saw it too. It says: WHEELCHAIR ACCESS. That means Bluish—and we get to go too. Missus says we can, me and Tuli and Bluish in the chair and her mom. Not that her mom's not nice. She's just kind of different than my family. But this is not about her.

We went to the side of the big steps and went under and through a big door. We went on in that way to an elevator. And up to the second floor. We meet the kids coming in and follow them.

"Where are we going?"

Man! It's the Great Hall of the Dinosaurs, we call it. Has this great big skeleton and murals like two stories high on each end. Story of peoples from different times.

Ms. Baker spoke about them. All these visiting fa-real big people going to different parts of the museum and getting tickets, paying money. Ms. Baker took care of us. We all stood together. Max put us in bunches 'cause we all can't go in at once. Too many of us.

"It's not a great big place," Max says.

"Well, where is it?"

"In the vivarium. It's a closed habitat."

We went into the Oceana Hall of Birds part, they call it. Where they put the vivarium.

They told us, "You have to get through the first doors quickly—don't let anything escape! Go through the next doors and you are in!" Her mom said, OK, I could wheel Bluish. I did! We get through the doors and we didn't let anything out.

Nobody minded that our ten bunch went first. Almost too many kids. Oh, it was hot.

"I want to stand." Bluish, she stood. Tuli sat in Bluish's chair. Paula pushed Tulifoolie. Funny! Bluish is just like anybody standing.

Always some of us have our caps on just like hers so nobody knows she's been sick. Bluish and us walking around looking at everything. It took her breath some but she loved it there. I let her take my arm, she is so very not heavy. Her mom watches. But I don't tell Bluish. It was so hot and wet in there it curled my hair!

They call it a made-up fragile forest in the middle of icy New York. Called it: Tropical Butterflies Alive in Winter, the official name. Not just any old butterflies too. But 500 great big ones and little ones from the tropics. 80 degrees in there! Whew! The humidity is way high too. Oh the butterflies, tropical plants, and rotting food—they like it!

One landed on Max's sweater.

We held out our arms. Butterflies came soon. It was so fun! Colors were so many! Pretty! Be gentle! So bright.

A big one landed on my shoulder. Then on Bluish, right on her arm. It was humongous!

"Max, Max! Look on Bluish!"

Bluish's eyes got great big. Her face lit up, man! She looked so happy.

"It's all blue!" she said.

"It's way big, too," Tuli said. "Ho-ney don't bring it near me. I'll scream if you do." But I watched Bluish. Her face filled. She was all happy. Butterfly giant.

Max says, reading: "It's a Blue Morpho with a b-i-i-i-g wingspan. It's a big butterfly!"

They told us not to brush the butterflies off us. Let them walk off or lead them onto a plant. Or we could hurt them.

"Butterflies are poisonous, toxic, most of them." Max was reading it.

Bluish stares at the Blue Morpho as it finds a plant. Looking so far away now. But I read her. I didn't look. Knew she was thinking, "Me, Bluish, toxic me."

"That don't mean nothing. You weren't born that way." I told it to the air.

The Morpho fluttered its wings open, then half-closed, like breathing out and in. Bluish wobbled. I got her chair for her. Her mom helped her and took Bluish out to the Great Hall.

I stayed in to watch all kinds—a Zebra

Swallowtail that looked like the animal. Orange ones and one little red-rimmed one. I read a pamphlet about all the butterflies. I'm going to put it up in my room so I'll know. Willie's going to want one, so I took two. I like the Isabella Tiger butterfly. It's so dainty. The Monarch looks small next to the big Blue Morpho.

There's something scary about that Morpho. Like it bites, maybe. All so bright and deadly, maybe. Border all black.

Going through the vivarium, all of us, didn't take more than an hour. You can't stand the humidity longer than 15 minutes. I gave a last look to the tropics. Giant green plants and a giant Blue Morpho.

Well, it was sure something. From egg to caterpillar to pupa—when the caterpillar doesn't eat or move. It rests and becomes an adult. The bitter/butter/fly!

We don't have time for the nature shop outside the vivarium. Shoot. But whoop! I got an idea…guess what?

CHAPTER SEVEN

All Us

Christmas was nice for Dreenie, but not the best thing she could think of. She never got what she really wanted. Willie got clothes, and things for her Game Boy. She got a really nice doll. Dreenie got a Barbie. She got the jeans she wanted. She got boots. They always got games from relatives.

It was all nice, she thought. *I helped decorate our tree two days before Christmas. But you don't always get what you want.*

She and Tuli waited to go back to Bluish's house before they all exchanged gifts. It was now two days after Christmas. Bluish had been out of town for the holiday.

They were at Bluish's house, in her room. They'd returned from the African Market at a near uptown school. The market had been fun: bright, colorful decorations, music and games, food. Bluish and her dad went with Dreenie and her dad, and Tuli. Next, both of Bluish's parents, Bluish, and Tuli would go over to Dreenie's house.

Dreenie had gotten Tuli different bands and clips for her hair. They came in a painted box. And Tuli tried them on, deftly pulling her hair back, up, or to the side. She looked in the mirror and smiled at herself.

Bluish's eyes nearly popped out of her head when she opened her present from Dreenie. "Oh! Oh! Wow!" she said. "Where did...?"

"Do you like it?"

"It's so cool, Dreen!"

It was the Blue Morpho, painted and crafted from a kind of plastic that felt soft and smooth. Dreenie had found it in the nature shop when she and her mom and dad took Willie to see the butterflies. "It looks exactly like the real one. Exactly the same size! I love it!" Bluish said. "Thank you, thank you!"

But no one was more surprised than Dreenie when she opened up her holiday gift from Bluish. "How'd you know?" Dreenie asked.

"Well, you didn't talk about anything else after the field trip," Bluish said.

It was the Isabella Tiger model, the butterfly Dreenie had liked best.

"Wow," Dreenie said. "Cool! I'm going to hang it in my room so it looks like it's flying." The Isabella Tiger wasn't as large as the Blue Morpho. Something about it reminded Dreenie of a lady's delicate fan.

"I'm going to hang mine, too," Bluish said.

Tuli powdered her face, using the compact Bluish had given her for Christmas. "The powder smells good," she said. "It's just my color, too."

Tuli had given Bluish and Dreenie each a CD of Christmas music. And now, Bluish's CD was playing in the living room, where everyone in the house could hear it. They listened as Nat "King" Cole sang, "Merry Christmas, toooo you...."

"My dad loves Christmas music," Bluish said.

"So does my mom," Dreenie said.

Tuli eyed them. "You don't like the CDs as much as you like the butterfly presents," she said.

"Oh, yes we do, too," Dreenie said. Everything was a test with Tuli.

Bluish said, "When I look at the Morpho, I feel like I can go anywhere and do anything. But I can't hear it! I can hear the Christmas music."

"Yeah! That's right!" Tuli said, but then she asked, "Is seeing better than hearing?"

"Tuli, stop," Dreenie told her. "All our presents are just right, so quit it."

"Anyway, you have the best coat of anybody," Bluish said. "I got a duffel coat for my Hanukkah-Christmas." She smiled. "I asked for it. My dad says I'm 'earthy-crunchy,' like my mom. He means I like outdoor stuff, winter and summer."

Dreenie got good presents for Christmas, but not what she really wanted. She didn't talk about it, but she said, "Nobody has a coat like yours, Tuli. Leather, with a real fake-fur collar? I mean, nobody but you!"

"I know it," Tuli said, delighted. "Never thought they'd get me something like this." She still had the coat on. It fit her perfectly, with the fur up close around her neck.

Tuli paraded up and down the room in her coat. She took the Blue Morpho out of its box and danced with it. Her bright hair sprang and tumbled around her face as she tossed her head.

Dreenie snatched the Morpho from her and pitched it over to Bluish on her bed. "It doesn't belong to you," she said to Tuli.

"I wasn't going to hurt it," Tuli said, flopping down in a chair.

Tuli's the prettiest, Dreenie thought. "That coat makes you look like a movie star," Dreenie told her.

"I wish I could look like that," Bluish said. "I don't look like much of nothing."

"Hey, I think you look good," Dreenie was quick to say to Bluish.

"I do, too," Tuli said.

Bluish lay curled sideways on her bed, her head on two pillows. "I always have to lie down, still."

"Yeah, but you walk more," Tuli said.

"Then I get tired longer," Bluish said. "I feel better...." She laced the large Blue Morpho through her fingers. But she didn't sound convinced. She sat up. "Listen, I hear my dad." Her dad was calling them. They headed down the hall. Bluish held on to a wooden bar along the wall. Dreenie had never seen anything like it before.

Bluish's mom stood by the door in a long, black duffel coat with a green plaid lining. She'd taken it out of the hall closet and put it on. She had Bluish's coat over her arm. She was beautiful in a grown-up way. *Different from Tuli*, Dreenie thought. *I'd sure like to be looking gorgeous like her someday. She has on nice makeup, too.*

Dreenie's dad had stayed a while, talking. He had brought them from the market. Mr. Winburn was saying that if he drove them home, Dreenie's dad wouldn't have to drive them back. And he said that he could take Tuli home, too. So it was agreed. They would go to Dreenie's house in two cars. Dreenie had felt jealous that Mr. Winburn offered Tuli a ride home. She didn't know why, exactly. *Don't be like that,* she told herself. She got to ride in Bluish's car. "You get to ride home with them later," she murmured to Tuli, "so let me ride with Bluish now." Tuli didn't mind riding with Dreenie's dad, so long as she got to go, and be with everybody.

Not many people on West End Avenue, Dreenie noticed, as they drove. It was cold out, but not snowy. What people she saw were all bundled up, dressed up in holiday clothes, she guessed. *Christmas is for family; so is Hanukkah,* she was thinking. *I'm glad it's gone, though.*

"Did you have fun at your grandmother's?" Dreenie asked quietly, only for Bluish to hear. They sat together in the backseat of the Winburns' car.

Bluish made a face. "My grandma *hovers,* like a helicopter," Bluish told her, right in her ear. "Mummy tells her, 'Don't hover over Natalie. She doesn't like it.' I hate it!"

"Guess she worries about you," Dreenie said.

"She keeps telling me how skinny I am. And made me weigh myself. I didn't want her to see so

I got off the scale before she could. Mummy was mad. I don't weigh much! Mummy told Grandma that we would leave if she didn't stop. Grandma presses on my arms and shoulders. I don't have any fat, and it hurts—my bones…"

"Sorry you didn't have a good time."

"Well, I did, mostly," Bluish said. "I got nice things for Hanukkah….My mom's relatives came. Aunt Millie and Uncle David, Mummy's brother. They have two boys, older. One's a freshman in college. They're always really nice to me. They talked to me like…like I am a person…not a sick person."

"We had fifteen people for Christmas dinner," Dreenie said. "My mom's sister came from Long Island City with her family. And my cousins came," Dreenie said. "Just my family. Not Tuli."

"You like Tuli? She had somewhere else to go?" asked Bluish.

"I like her. But it was Christmas. I…don't like having to take care of her so much. I can't help worrying about her granmom. They went to her aunt's."

Bluish stared at Dreenie. "You worry about me, don't you?"

"Yeah, but that's different."

"You worry about me because I'm sick."

"No!"

"Yes."

"No! I mean, I want to help—I mean, be your friend."

"You don't want to help Tuli?"

Dreenie sighed, and thought about it. "I wish she didn't need me all the time. I wish she'd depend on herself. Maybe I'm wrong…"

Bluish had been looking right into Dreenie's face. Now she looked straight ahead. "I think you and I are a lot alike," she said.

"I think so, too," Dreenie said. "My mom says you have to care about people, if you want people to care about you."

"When I was real sick, I thought I didn't care about anything," Bluish said. "I thought for sure I wanted everything to be over." She stopped. "Let's not—" She broke off, looking out the window. Her mood had changed.

Dreenie tried smiling, humming Christmas music. But Bluish frowned and leaned farther away. She stared out the window the rest of the time, leaving Dreenie wondering what she'd done wrong.

At the apartment, Dreenie's mom had everything really nice. Willie stood in the doorway as they came in. She looked cute in her Christmas jeans and new sweater. New Air Jordans.

"Everybody, we have to do introductions!" Willie announced loudly.

"Oh, Willie! Mom, tell her to calm down." Dreenie was completely embarassed. They weren't even out of their coats.

"Dreen, it's okay. Willie, help take people's coats," her mom said.

Mrs. Winburn was smiling. "Hi, Willie," she said. "Merry Christmas."

"Hi, Mrs. Winburn. Happy Hanukkah!" Willie said, like she said the greeting every day. Maybe she did, Dreenie thought. Nothing shy about Willie!

Dreenie's dad introduced her mom to Bluish's mom and dad.

"Pleased to meet you. I'm Anneva," Dreenie's mom said, extending her hand to the Winburns.

"And I'm Natalie," Bluish said to Dreenie's mom. She was standing. Mr. Winburn folded her chair and lay it in a corner. "All the kids like to call me Bluish!" Bluish said. She glanced at her mom and shook hands with Dreenie's mom.

"I'm glad to meet you, Natalie. I like your hat!" Dreenie's mom said. "I heard you made them for all the kids in your class. That's just great!"

Mrs. Winburn smiled, pleased.

They all took off their coats for Willie and Dreenie to carry to the bedroom. Everyone had a chance to admire Tuli's new coat before she took it off. There was something about Tuli that made you want to give her compliments, Dreenie decided.

Her mom was saying how great the coat looked on Tuli. "I wish I could get a coat to look like that on me!" They all laughed.

They went to the living room. The table was set, and they would have food later. Next, Dreenie's mom explained to everyone that Kwanzaa was a new celebration for them. One that was fun and interesting. "We always celebrate Christmas. This is something new and informative. We light seven candles."

"We light candles for the Hanukkah holidays," Bluish said. "It's my mom's tradition. We have Christmas, too."

"I like the idea of candles even when it's not a holiday celebration," Dreenie's mom said. And she began by lighting the black candle in the center of the kinara of the Kwanzaa candelabra. "This represents *Umoja*, the first principle of Kwanzaa," her mom said. "It means unity and helps us work together in our family, in our community, and in our nation."

"That's very important," Mrs. Winburn said.

"I like that the best," Willie said.

Dreenie's mom and dad both took up explaining how the red and green candles and the black one in the center symbolized the seven principles of Kwanzaa. They tried not to sound as if they were giving a lesson, but they did. Mr. and Mrs.

Winburn, Bluish, Tuli, Willie, and Dreenie all got to light a candle. As they did, Dreenie's dad told them what each candle stood for. "*Ujima*, the first candle, work and responsibility. *Kujichagulia*, the first red candle, for self-determination. All these words are Swahili words. This is a seven-day ceremony starting on December 26 and going through January 1. By lighting all the candles, we demonstrate the ceremony and the meaning."

"It has many parts," Dreenie's mom continued. "It's a celebration of past, present, and future. A proverb is often quoted: 'I am because we are; because we are, I am.'"

"Oh, that's lovely," Mrs. Winburn said.

Her mom and dad explained more until, finally, her mom said, "I'll leave the candles burning. Let's have dinner! You all come to the table."

Everybody oohed and ahhhed over the dinner. Her mom had called and invited Bluish's family to come. The dinner was like a traditional holiday feast. Lots of food, only instead of turkey, there were breaded herring filets. Baked chicken.

Wonderful baked corn. Salad, white beans and red beans, and black-eyed peas. Cake and ice cream.

"Have you ever seen children pile their plates so high?" Dreenie's dad said.

At first, Bluish seemed hungry. She ate the fish and corn. She didn't want salad. She had a table-spoonful of the white beans.

"You did good!" Willie told Bluish.

"You did!" Dreenie told her.

"It smells so good!" Bluish said. But she didn't smile. She stared at all of them, their heaping plates. And looked as if she might be getting sick.

Her mom kept her lips tightly sealed and tried not to watch her daughter.

No one expected Willie, Dreenie, Tuli, and Bluish to sit and talk with their parents over coffee. In their room, Willie showed them her different Game Boy games. Bluish sat in a chair. She looked tired. "You can lie on my bed," Dreenie said.

"I don't need to," spoken almost in a whisper.

"Yes, you do," Dreenie said.

"Here, I gonna carry you," Tuli said, joking

lightly. Bluish didn't object to Tuli and Dreenie helping her out of the chair.

"I coulda done it by myself!" Bluish said. Her mouth turned down. Her face screwed up, as if she had a bad taste in her mouth. She lay still on her back on the pillows. Willie closed the door.

"You feel bad?" Dreenie asked her. She came over and kneeled beside the bed.

Tears seeped out of the corners of Bluish's eyes. "Not the way you think I feel bad," she said. And then she cried with her mouth wide open. It was an awful-sounding cry.

"What hurts you?" Dreenie asked, alarmed. "Please don't cry!"

"Shall I call her mom?" Tuli asked.

"No, don't," Bluish said, gasping. "I get like this...."

They waited, watching her. Willie came up, touched Bluish on her cap.

Dreenie got some tissues. Bluish wiped her face with them. "It...takes just so long, to get like you guys again."

"Are you going to die?" Willie asked.

"Willie!" Dreenie was outraged. She almost slapped her little sister. Made a move to do something to her, when Bluish said, "Don't. It's okay."

"You ain't gonna die, no time," Tuli said. "Nuh-uh, ho-ney, not with us around!"

Dead silence. And then, Bluish giggled. Dreenie laughed. Tuli always could make them laugh.

"We won't let anything bad happen to you," Dreenie said with a lump in her throat. She nearly cried herself. She held Bluish's trembling hands, so small and bony.

"Let's make a pact!" Willie said.

"Yeah!" Tuli said. "How you do that?"

"I know," Dreenie said at once. "Everybody hold hands."

Bluish turned somewhat on her side. Dreenie and Tuli held her hands, and held Willie's. Suddenly, it came to Dreenie. The proverb her mom had recited sounded in her mind. Dreenie made one for them: "Bluish is, because we are; we are, because Bluish—is—us!"

"We, us," Willie said.

"We, us." They all said it.

Bluish whispered it, "We, us." Then they lifted their hands and let go.

They stayed in the room, close, talking, sometimes laughing. Bluish sat up. She didn't look at them. Then she reached up and took off her knit cap.

They stared.

Silence, until Willie gurgled.

Dreenie's mouth fell open. She screeched; she and Tuli screamed. And laughed! Peals of laughter.

Willie spun around and around. "Oh, muh goodness!" she said.

"Bluish!" Tuli said.

"No! No! Reddish!" Dreenie hollered.

They jumped up and down. "You have hair!" Dreenie shouted. It had to be the shortest copper-red hair anybody'd ever seen.

"Looks just like peach fuzz," Willie said.

"No, it's shiny, and curlier than fuzz. It's gonna be ringlets. It's cute!" Dreenie said. "Bluish!"

"No, Reddish!" They all yelled it at once. And the color of a new penny. Hollering and laughing, until Dreenie's mom knocked and opened the door, to see what in the world was going on.

JOURNAL

A Record Of Bluish—It's A New Year

Nobody knows about this journal but me. I write in it when Willie's watching her TV shows. I hide it in my drawer that locks.

I guess I always meant to give it to you. Only I didn't know till now. See, because the only way it's right to have it and still be friends is if you own it.

This journal never was about me. This record of Bluish is YOURS. I'm giving it over to you to keep or throw away. A record from the very first time I saw you. I didn't mean this to be bad. Not for you to be real mad at me—I hope not. We walk right in to the New Year—Dreanne and Natalie. GFF. Good Friends Forever.

And you don't know it yet, but I got something special for Christmas. Only, after Christmas. My dad said he would get me one big special gift! He knew what I wanted. But I didn't get it for Christmas. I was so sad! But I never said a word to him that I didn't get it.

But I did! I did! On New Year's Eve I got home from Tuli's after school. We went and got her night-clothes and stuff. Tuli had to spend the night to watch Times Square. She just wouldn't take no! I should have called you, but I didn't know she was coming. We go to my room. And guess what? GUESS! You can't!

A DOG! A real little PUPPY! All mine! Not Willie's. Not anybody else's. You and me can walk our dogs when it's summer. Pretty dark brown with kind of white patches. Spaniel, they call it. It's a girl! She has her own bed.

I get to run home at lunch and pet her and feed her, Mommy says. Daddy says we have to train her.

Will you help me?

Right now Poochie is asleep on my lap. Little sweet Poochie. You like that name? I think it's nice. Here comes Willie to bother me.

So this is it. I signed my name, see? *Dreenie.*

End of journal.

I'll bring it over.

I hope we can still be friends.

I have another one to write. This one has to start out earlier. Guess who? Hint—Movie Star. Leather....

Then I'll do mine.